GREEN POWER

Earth-Friendly Energy Through the Ages

A. G. Smith

DOVER PUBLICATIONS, INC.
Mineola, New York

We live at a time of growing worldwide concern that the burning of carbon-based fossil fuels (coal and oil) is polluting our environment and contributing to global warming. As the use of these fuels expands and the damage continues, the need to find alternatives becomes more urgent. This coloring book depicts the developments and uses of these "Green Energy" resources, while providing engaging coloring pages.

Sources of energy such as windmills and waterwheels are in tune with the elements. In times past, wind power and water power were used to grind grain, run sawmills, and operate spinning machines. In agriculture, windmills were used to pump water and to drain and irrigate fields.

Today, modern windmills and hydroelectric turbines generate electricity to power almost all aspects of our lives. What is more important is that these power sources are non-polluting, and there is still clean water and wind when all is done.

Passive solar energy—the heat of the sun—was used in ancient times to heat buildings and dry food for storage. Today, many of us use the sun's heat to dry clothes on lines in our backyards. In recent years the development of solar cells and more efficient batteries have allowed us to collect and store energy from the sun as needed. The use of hydrogen, created from water— H_2O —also is being developed as a source of non–carbon-based energy.

Bibliographical Note

Green Power: Earth-Friendly Energy Through the Ages is a new work, first published by Dover Publications, Inc., in 2010.

DOVER *Pictorial Archive* SERIES

This book belongs to the Dover Pictorial Archive Series. You may use the designs and illustrations for graphics and crafts applications, free and without special permission, provided that you include no more than four in the same publication or project. (For permission for additional use, please write to Permissions Department, Dover Publications, Inc., 31 East 2nd Street, Mineola, N.Y. 11501.)

However, republication or reproduction of any illustration by any other graphic service, whether it be in a book or in any other design resource, is strictly prohibited.

International Standard Book Number
ISBN-13: 978-0-486-47447-2
ISBN-10: 0-486-47447-X

Manufactured in the United States by Courier Corporation
47447X01
www.doverpublications.com

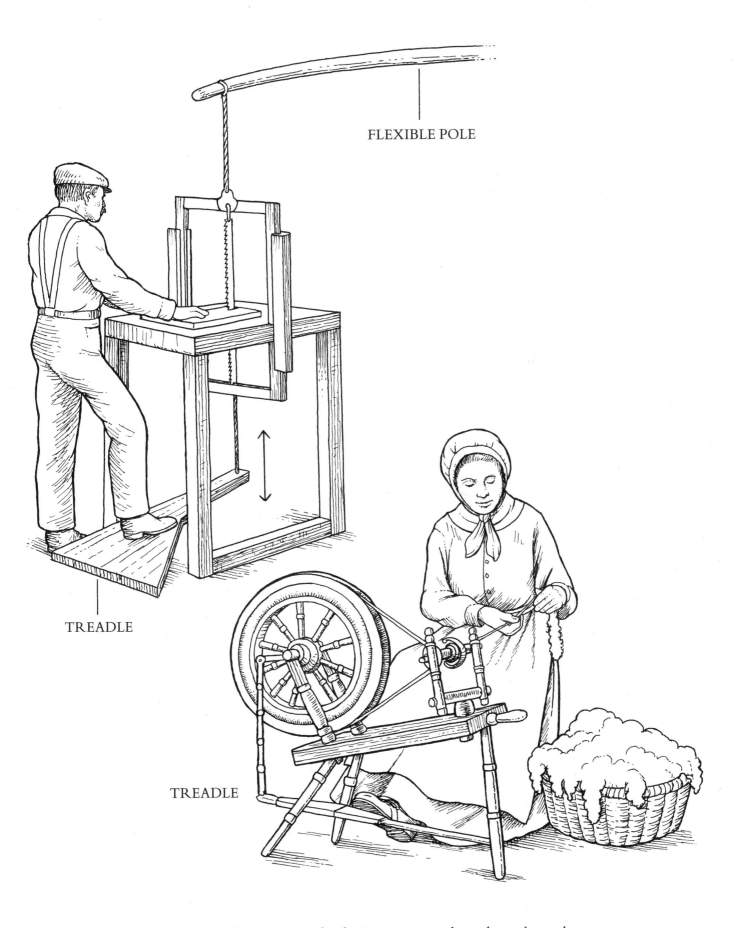

FLEXIBLE POLE

TREADLE

TREADLE

The pole saw and spinning wheel. Our ancestors devised simple machines to make everyday tasks easier. The spring in the flexible pole supplies energy to the saw. The momentum of the wheel drives the spindle.

1

The treadmill. Both human and animal power have been used to drive treadmills. In medieval times, large wooden cranes powered treadmills on wharves. They were often covered to protect them from the weather.

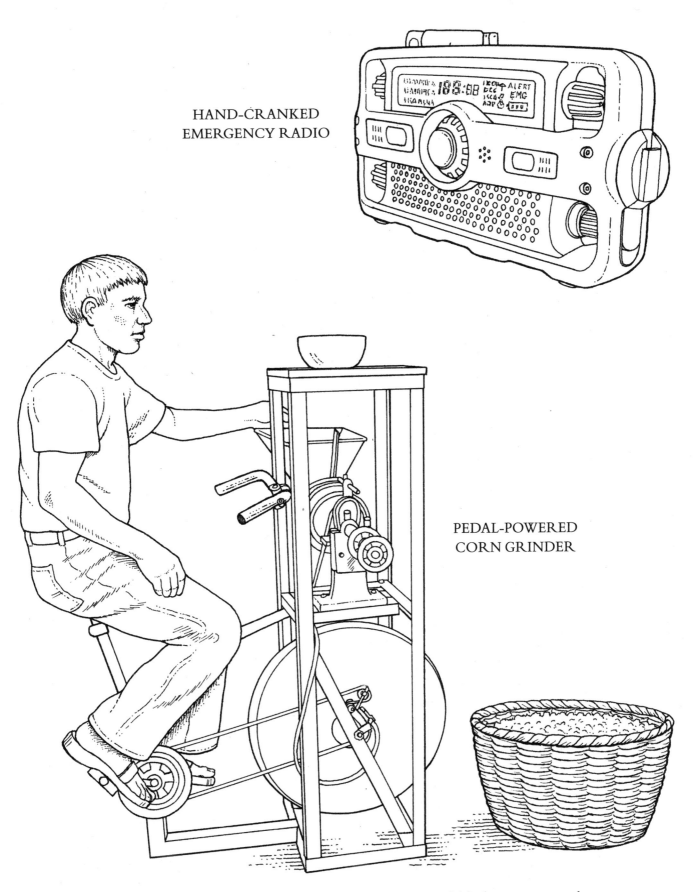

HAND-CRANKED
EMERGENCY RADIO

PEDAL-POWERED
CORN GRINDER

Modern human power. In places where electricity is unavailable, human-powered devices are popular. The hand-cranked radio is useful during power outages. The pedal-powered corn grinder is used in remote villages in Central America that have no electricity.

The horse-powered windlass. The horse is harnessed to a shaft on the upper level of this sixteenth-century mine. The gears on the middle level transfer energy to a horizontal shaft, which is attached to a chain raising a leather ore bucket.

The vertical-shaft water mill. The corn is fed into a hopper. The horizontal water wheel turns a vertical shaft, driving the movable millstone. The wheel can be disengaged by lifting a beam. These examples are from Macedonia.

Undershot water wheels. This Roman mill plant used a single water source to drive fourteen undershot waterwheels. The plant was erected at Barbegal (Italy) in the early fourth century A.D.

The water-powered forge. This seventeenth-century smithy used a single undershot waterwheel to drive a trip-hammer and a pair of bellows. Follow the power train from the well to the furnace.

The overshot water wheel. This arrangement shows an overshot wheel with the
water supply diverted. The miller needed only to turn a shaft inside the mill to raise
a sluice gate, allowing the water to flow over the wheel.

The steel overshot water wheel. During the nineteenth century, the use of iron and steel wheels greatly improved the efficiency of water-powered technology. Many innovative devices were patented.

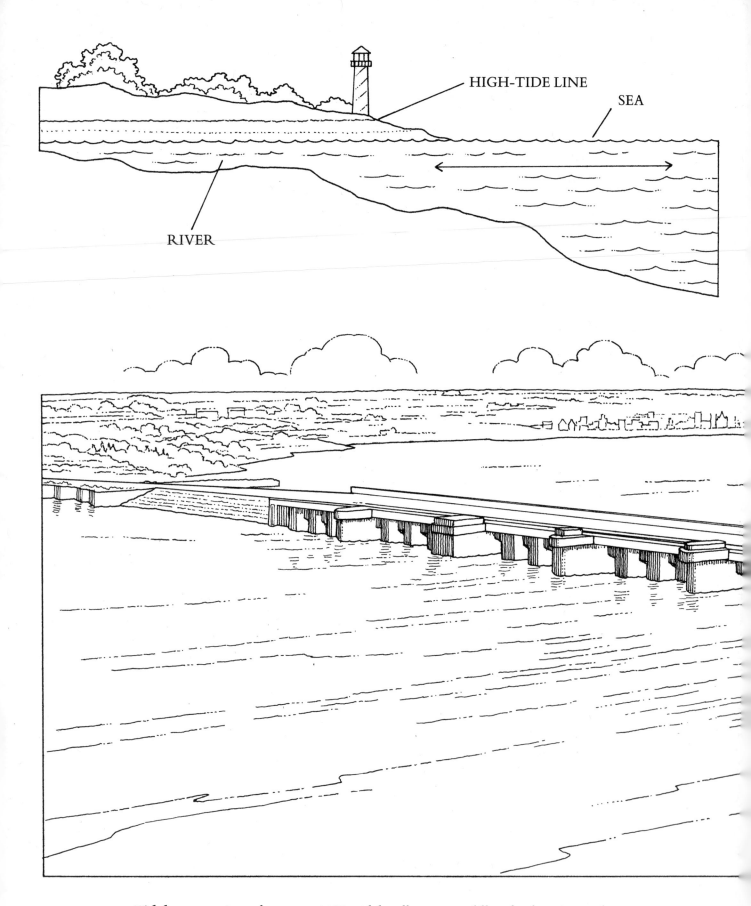

HIGH-TIDE LINE

SEA

RIVER

Tidal power. As early as A.D. 1100, tidal mills using paddle wheels were used to grind corn in Britain and France. The rising and falling of tides was also used as a power source in colonial America. Small dams were built on tidal basins, and the receding water was used to power small mills.

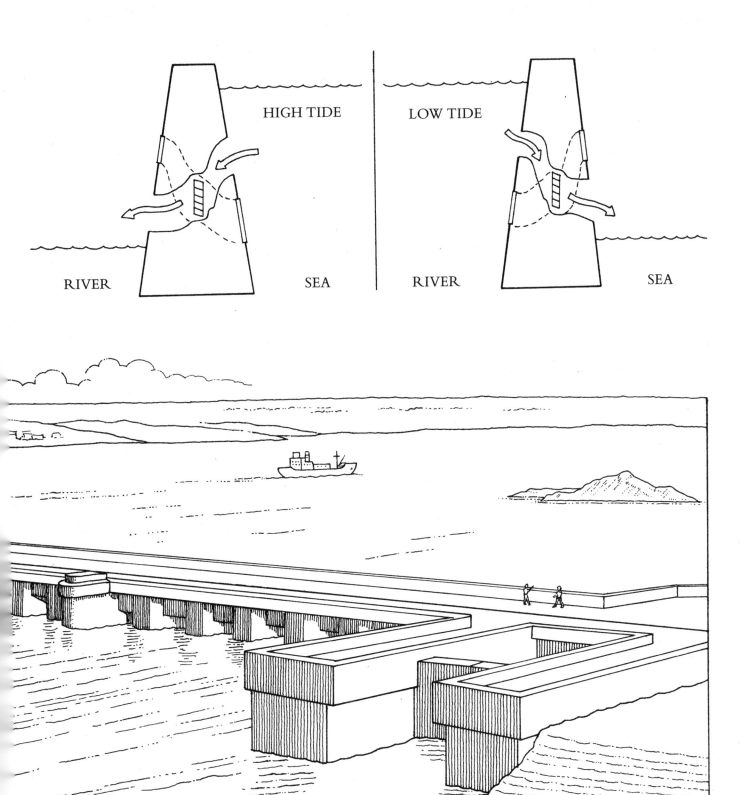

HIGH TIDE LOW TIDE

RIVER SEA RIVER SEA

Modern tidal power plants employ sophisticated reversing turbines that take advantage of both the ebb and flow of the tidal cycle. Electricity is generated by the turbines.

11

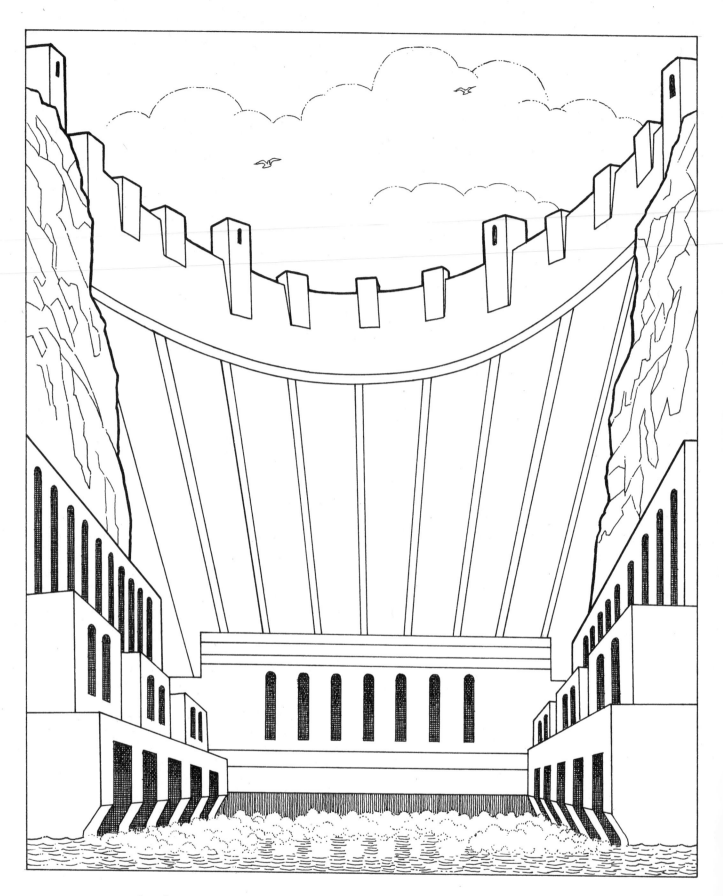

Hydroelectric power plants. With the widespread use of electric power in the twentieth century, flowing water became an important natural resource. Great rivers were dammed and their power harnessed to drive modern water turbines generating electricity.

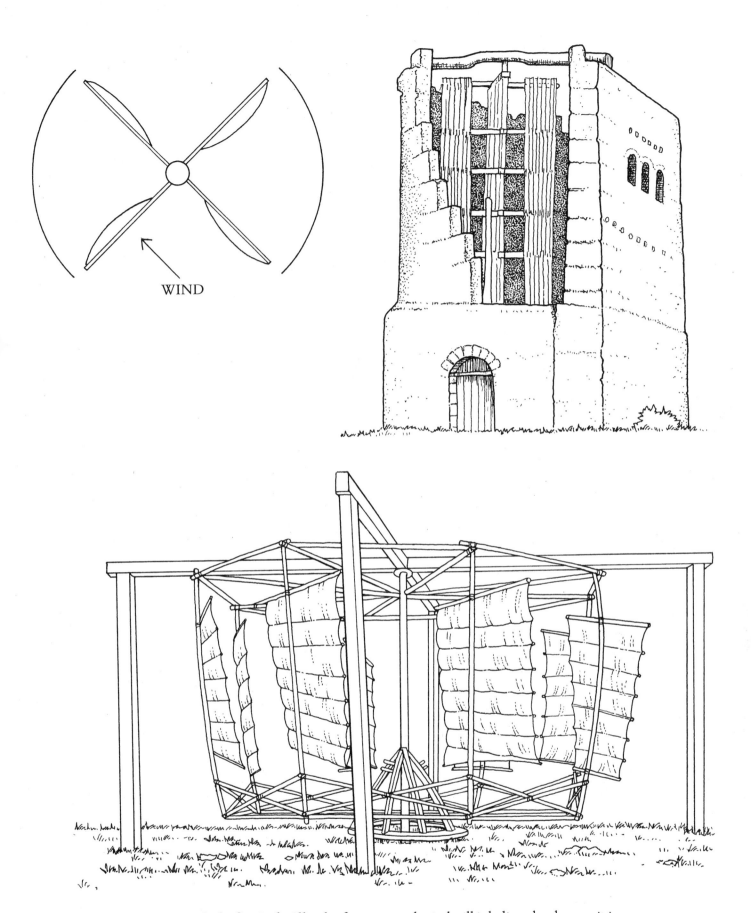

WIND

The vertical-shaft windmill. The first practical windmill is believed to have originated in Persia (modern-day Iran) in the seventh century A.D. A vertical shaft drove a millstone directly. In China lightly built vertical-shaft windmills are still used with chain plumb for irrigation. Earlier types would have been built of bamboo.

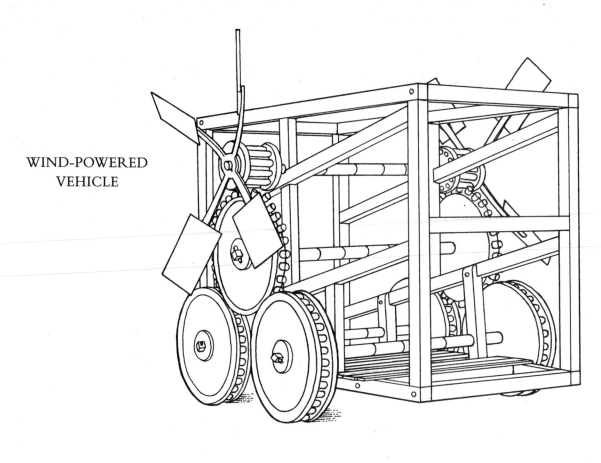

WIND-POWERED
VEHICLE

WIND-POWERED
ORGAN

Whimsical experiments. This wind-powered pipe organ was described by Hero of Alexandria in his manuscript "Pneumatica" in the second century B.C. The wind-powered vehicle was designed during the Renaissance by an Italian engineer, Robertos Valturio (? –1484). Although such experiments proved to be impractical, they often led to further developments.

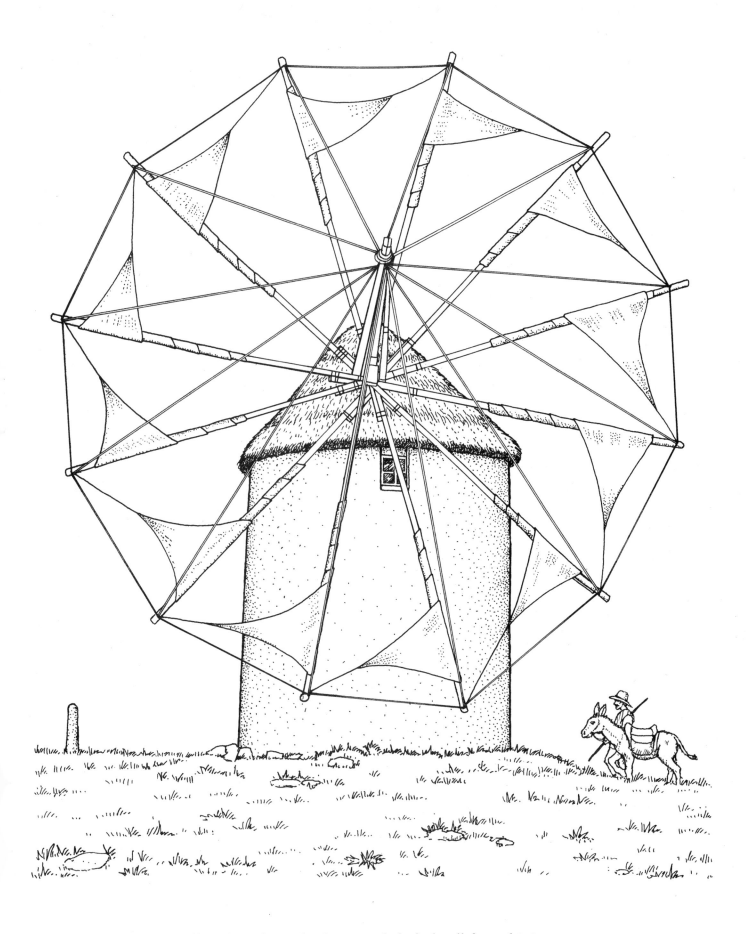

Tower mills. The sails on this horizontal-shafted mill from the Aegean region appear to have been directly inspired by the lateen sails of early Mediterranean ships. By the fourteenth century such windmills were common in Europe.

The post mill. The problem of keeping the sails or blades facing the wind was first solved by the post mill. The mill was suspended around a large center post, and the entire mill was turned to face the wind by means of a tiller.

The smock mill. As mills became larger, the problem of blade direction was solved by turning only the cap of the mill to face the wind. This Dutch polder mill is also described as a smock mill because of the resemblance of the tower form to a dress or "smock."

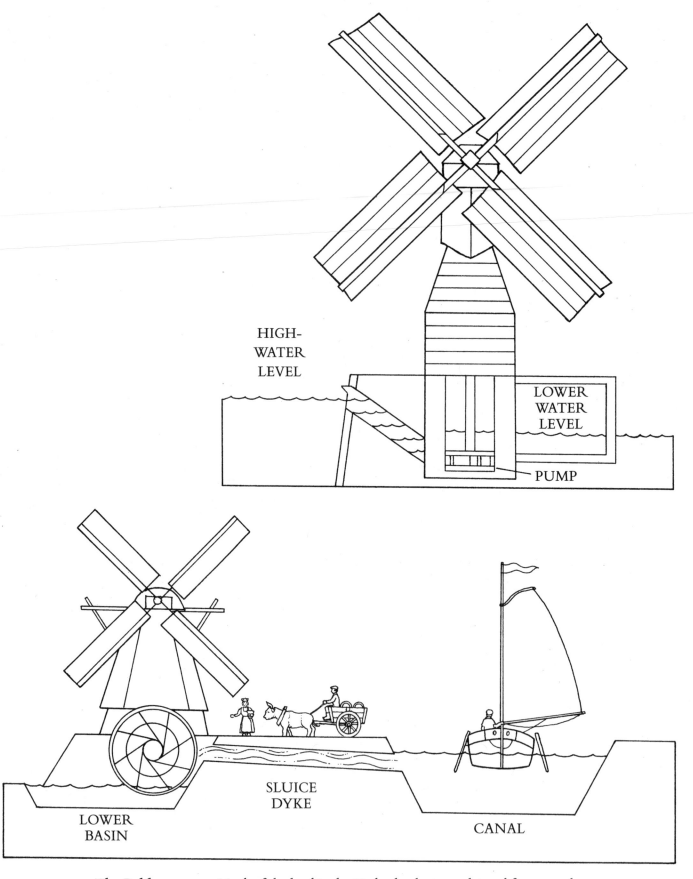

HIGH-
WATER
LEVEL

LOWER
WATER
LEVEL

PUMP

SLUICE
DYKE

LOWER
BASIN

CANAL

The Polder system. Much of the land in the Netherlands was reclaimed from marsh-land and the sea. Beginning in the sixteenth century, a series of dykes were methodically designed and constructed. The low-lying areas surrounded by the dykes, called polders, were kept drained by pumps powered by large and small windmills.

Modern wind turbines. In the latter part of the twentieth century, as societies recognized the finite limits to and the destructive consequences of burning fossil fuels, engineers have reconsidered windmills as a clean source of energy. Today, "wind farms" with rows of modern wind-powered turbines supply electricity to many towns and cities.

Sailing ships—old and new. Humans began using cloth sails to catch the wind and propel small vessels more than three thousand years ago. Recently, modern ships with "sails" controlled by computers have been developed. The example shown here is the *Shin Aitoku Maru*, a Japanese coastal tanker fitted with rectangular auxiliary sails.

SUMMER

WINTER

Passive solar energy—Mesa Verde. We feel warm when we stand in the sunshine, and cool when we stand in the shade. The cliff dwellers of the American Southwest built their stone and clay houses along the edges of caves. When the sun was highest in the summer, they were sheltered from its hot rays. In winter, when the sun was lowest, they were warmed.

Modern environmental design. Today, many architects design houses to take advantage of both passive and active solar features. These include orientation: (1) shelter on the north side by a hillside and evergreen trees; (2) deeply inset windows and solarium with upper ventilation; and (3) active solar electric panels along the roof for power.

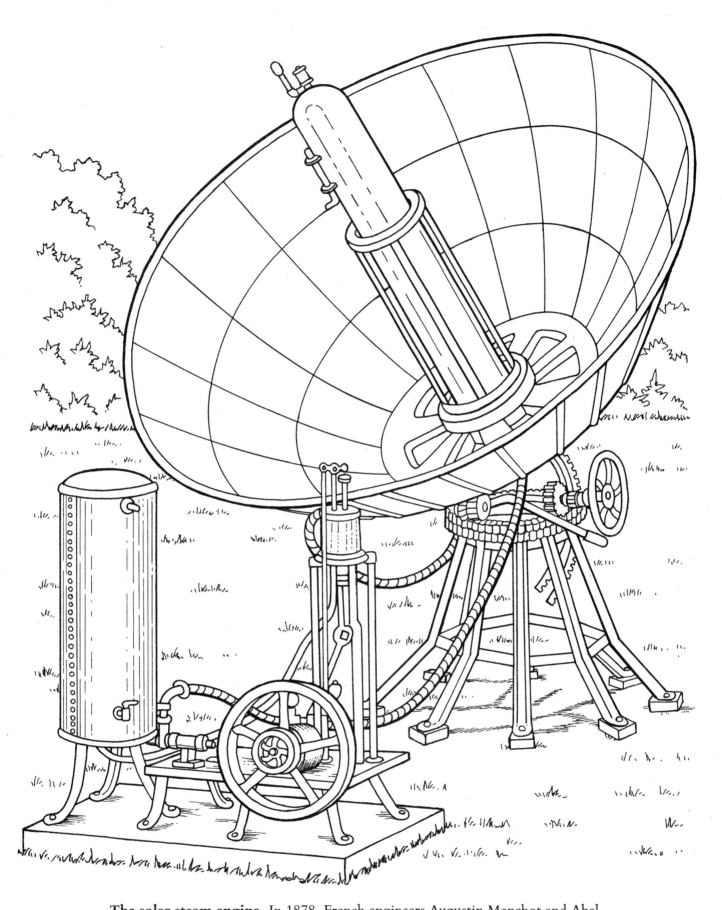

The solar steam engine. In 1878, French engineers Augustin Monchot and Abel
Pifre exhibited a solar-powered steam engine. A silver-plated copper disc reflected
the sun's rays onto the black-painted cylindrical boiler. The steam generated flow
through a tube back to a piston, driving the engine.

Solar furnaces. A solar furnace was built in Odeillo, France, in the 1960s. It incorporated a parabolic mirror on the side of an eleven-story building. The reflected radiation was focused on a solar collector at a temperature of 4,000° Centigrade. It generated 1,000 kilowatts of electricity.

SUN'S RAYS

FUEL CELL

Solar cells. In the late 1950s, silicon cells were developed in the United States. The solar cell consists of semi-conductors made of silicon crystals that have the ability to transform the sun's radiation into electricity. An early application of solar cells was supplying power to remote devices such as telecommunications relays.

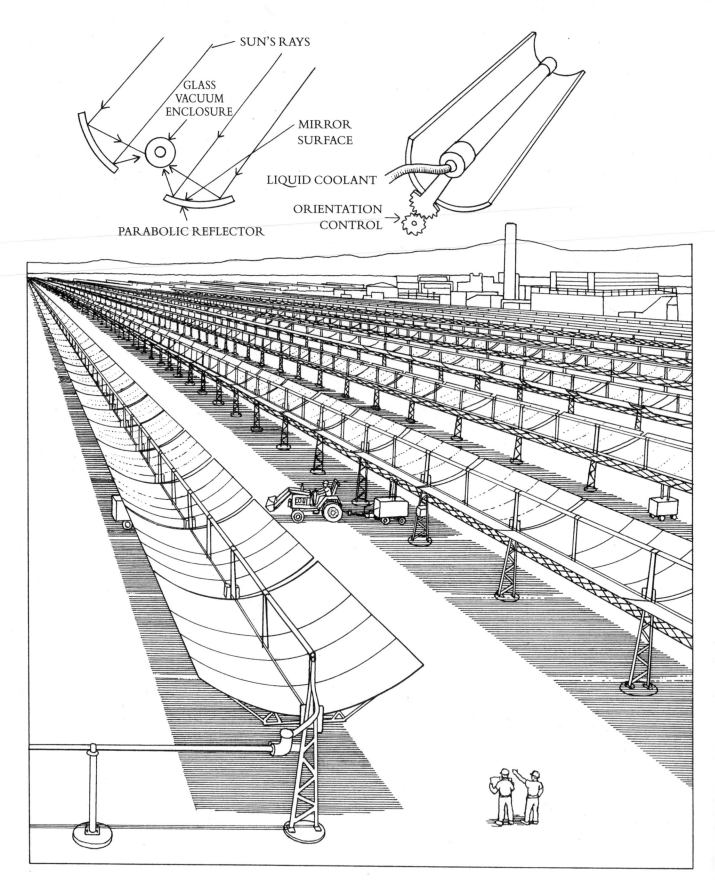

SUN'S RAYS

GLASS
VACUUM
ENCLOSURE

MIRROR
SURFACE

LIQUID COOLANT

ORIENTATION
CONTROL

PARABOLIC REFLECTOR

Solar power generation plants. In the world's sunnier and drier regions, such as California, Spain, and the Middle East, large commercial solar power plants have been constructed. These plants, covering many acres of desert, use mirrored collectors to focus the sun's rays on tubes of liquid pumped to steam generators, creating electric power. Other solar power plants employ acres of solar electric panels.

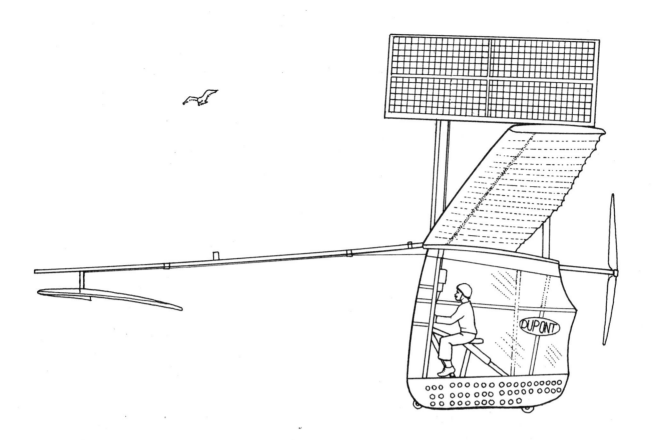

Electric transportation. In the late 1970s, a piloted ultra-light aircraft, the *Gossamer Penguin*, used power from solar cells to make experimental flights. Electric-powered automobiles are not new—this 1914 model, produced by the Anderson Electric Car Company (later the Detroit Electric Car Company), was powered by batteries.

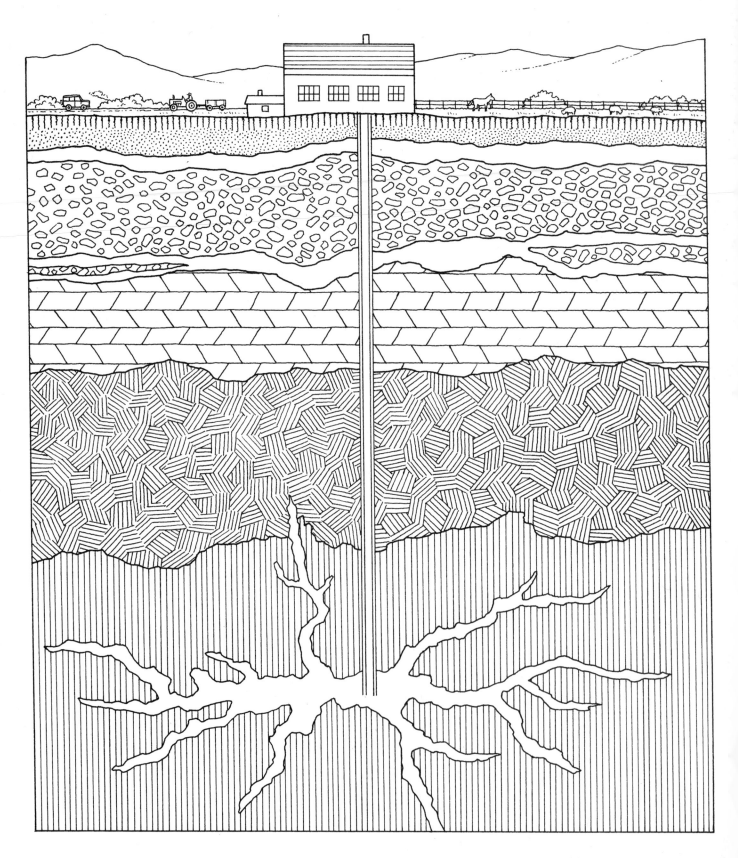

Geothermal energy. Energy may be obtained from the heat of the earth's core in the form of hot water or steam. Simple systems can be used to heat individual homes. These heat–pump systems are now widely in use.

Geothermal power plants. In areas of considerable volcanic activity—around the Pacific Rim, Iceland, and Italy—commercial geothermal plants have been built. This plant in Larderello, Italy, generates 400,000 kilowatts of electricity. The cooling towers dissipate steam.

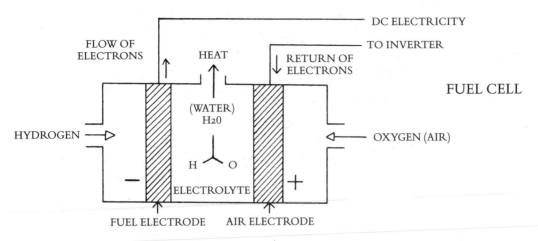

DC ELECTRICITY

FLOW OF
ELECTRONS

TO INVERTER

HEAT

RETURN OF
ELECTRONS

FUEL CELL

(WATER)
H_2O

HYDROGEN

OXYGEN (AIR)

H   O

−   +

ELECTROLYTE

FUEL ELECTRODE   AIR ELECTRODE

Fuel cells. Hydrogen fuel cells are virtually pollution free. They combine pure hydrogen and air to produce energy. Fuel cells have been used to power commercial buses on an experimental basis in several European and North American cities.